I0782233

MIRACLE ON THE *Mountain*

An Appalachian Christmas

Written by
Gail Heath

Illustrated by Barabash Sviatoslav

CONDOR PUBLISHING, INC.

LINCOLN, MICHIGAN

MIRACLE ON THE MOUNTAIN: An Appalachian Christmas

August 2025

All Rights Reserved. No part of this publication may be reproduced in any form or by any means, including scanning, photocopying, or otherwise without prior written permission of the copyright holder.

Copyright © 2025 by Gail Heath

Library of Congress Control Number: 2025941382

Illustrations by Barabash Sviatoslav
Illustrations and all rights owned by Condor Publishing, Inc.

All rights reserved

ISBN-13: 978-1-931079-67-9 (Paperback)
ISBN-13: 978-1-931079-68-6 (Hard Cover)

CONDOR PUBLISHING, INC.
PO Box 39 / 123 South Barlow
Lincoln, MI 48742
www.condorpublishinginc.com

Dedication

For my mother, Lucille MacDermaid,
and Dorothy Haley,
our cousin and lifelong friend.

Your love, wisdom,
and voices live on in Granny.

This story is for you—
with all my heart.

"Shep! Here, boy! Come on back!" Granny called. "It's too cold t'night. Be a good dawg, and don't you run away."

The old woman steadied herself with her walking stick, cupped one hand to her ear, and listened. Hemlock boughs creaked and rustled nearby, and snow swished softly beneath her boots. But Shep didn't answer.

"Okay," she said quietly. "Go on if ya have ta. I can't stop ya anyhow."

The wind whipped the hem of her wool coat as she stepped carefully along the trail. Slivers of moonlight flickered between the trees, casting long, dancing shadows across the glittering snow.

Skirting around a massive boulder, the woman nearly collided with a young man. He walked hunched over, pulling a wooden sled loaded with firewood, his ax tied securely on top of the logs.

"Howdy, Granny!" the youth greeted wearily. "What you doin' out this frosty night?"

"Why, Pete," she exclaimed with a warm smile, "you gave me quite a start. Didn't expect anybody on the path."

She pointed at the lights far down the mountain. "I'm headin' to service in the village. You oughta come, too—Christmas Eve an' all."

The boy gave a tired laugh and shook his head. "Ain't got time, Granny. Gotta get this wood delivered to folks, or their young'uns won't be havin' warm doin's 'round their Christmas trees come mornin'. Then I gotta skedaddle home and stoke the fire for Grandpappy."

"How's Henry doin'? I've not seen your granddaddy since that boar got him. Hurt him pretty bad, I hear."

"Yes, ma'am." The boy bit his lip and looked away. "He was tore up somethin' fierce. I just don't know, Granny. I just don't know. Sometimes it seems there ain't no hope."

"Such a pity. But, Pete, don't you be givin' up," said the woman. She reached out and hugged the lad.

He rubbed his eyes with his coat sleeve but didn't say anything.

"Say," Granny said, "you happen to see my hound go past? He runs off every Christmas Eve. He's no account—don't look like much, but he's a good ol' dawg. Wouldn't want to lose him. He was kinda my Christmas present 'bout ten years ago."

"Hain't seen no critters—too cold," said Pete, clearing his throat. "They're all hunkered down. Keepin' warm, I guess. Hope you find your dawg, Granny. Really sad to lose a hound; they's family."

"No worry. He's done this afore. Seems every Christmas Eve, just like tonight, as I'm a-fixin' to go down to the village for service, Shep takes off.

"I'm thinkin' I know where he went. He scooted up the mountain to an old fallen-down shack. It'll be late, but I'll swing by an' fetch him after service."

Granny looked up at the sky, her face glowing. "Isn't this a beautiful evenin', Pete? Tonight's my favorite of all nights— Christmas Eve."

Still straining at the weight of his loaded sled, Pete glanced up and nodded. "Yes, ma'am. It's a right pretty sky."

"Bet it was clear like this in Bethlehem," Granny said, smiling. "Though I don't reckon there was any frost in the air or snow on the ground. Can't you just imagine it? Angels

swoopin' down, singin' 'Glory to God in the highest.' Just the thought of it gives me the shivers."

Pete stopped, took a deep breath, and stepped back to his sled to tighten the rope holding the wood.

"Look!" Granny added in an awe-struck voice. "There's the Christmas star! Can you believe it's the same star that looked down on the stable that night of miracles?"

The tired young woodcutter nodded. "So they say," he muttered. "So they say."

"Don't you believe in miracles, Pete?" asked the woman. "This bein' the Christmas season an' all—the time of unexplained happenin's."

"Can't say as I do," replied the lad, his voice sharp. "Ain't seen any that I know 'bout. Not in my life."

Granny looked into the boy's eyes, her face softening with sadness. She reached out and patted his arm. "Whew," she exclaimed. "I'm kinda tired. I'm not so young anymore. You look plumb tuckered out yourself. Tell you what—I got me a jar o' hot chicory an' some cold biscuits here in my basket, enough for both of us. Let's rest a spell."

The old woman pointed to a large rock and a tree stump.

"I'll brush the snow off, and we'll sit," she said. "I want to tell ya what happened one Christmas Eve, years ago, right here on this ol' mountain. Took place long afore you an' your grandpappy came to live hereabouts."

Granny placed her basket on the snowy ground and took out a cloth bundle. Carefully, she unwrapped a Mason jar and a tin cup. She unscrewed the lid, poured steaming liquid into the cup, and handed it—along with a soft biscuit—to the boy.

"You know," she said, her voice barely more than a whisper, "there was a time I wasn't rightly certain I believed in miracles neither—'specially after I got one o' them telegrams about my boy Otis dyin' on some beach way over in France."

Granny fell silent, sitting quietly for a good long spell, eyes fixed on the bright star. Finally, she swallowed hard and looked back at Pete.

"But," she continued after a pause, her voice strong again, "I reckon I sure do now. Let me start at the beginnin'."

Pete held the cup close, steam warming his face as his eyes fixed on Granny. Her voice slowed, taking on a gentle, almost mystical rhythm. She began—softly, thoughtfully.

It musta been nigh close to ten years ago, or a bit more. I was at my little cabin over yonder, beyond that first ridge.

The old woman pointed into the darkness.

I had me a hatchet and was busy choppin' kindlin', jist mindin' my own business. Sudden like, I heard this fierce, boomin' voice behind me: "Old woman, what you doin'? You stop that commotion this minute, if'n ya know what's good fer ya, ya hear? You're scarin' off all the wildlife on the mountain!"

Well, I jumped so high I 'bout disconnected from my body—like a lizard when you grab him by the tail. I turned 'round and there stood the biggest and most ornery–lookin' character I ever did see. A little brown an' white puppy dog was cowerin' behind him. That man looked mean and hateful, and his eyes glared like burnin' coals—oh, how they glared. He appeared so frightenin', he even scared a garter snake back into its hole.

Granny looked at Pete.

"You ever know anybody with that much anger in 'em?" she asked.

The boy shook his head, lifted the warm cup, and took another sip.

Granny's eyes narrowed as she shook her head. "Now, Pete—this mountain's been my home since I was a young'un, and what that interloper claimed kinda aggravated me. Wouldn't you feel the same if'n it was you?"

"Yes, ma'am!" exclaimed the young man. "Reckon I sure would."

So I said to that rude feller, "Why, mister, who are you? I've never seen you afore. I'm Granny—everybody knows Granny. I been 'round here a long time. I don't mind sharin', but this mountain and that little cabin is my home. How about comin' along nice n' friendly? I'll pour you a cup of chicory."

"My name's Luster," he snarled. "An' don't you forget it! Don't want no chicory. And don't want none o' your hos–pi-tal-i-ty. I'm tellin' ya again, this here is my mountain now, my woods—an' if'n I feel kindly towards ya, I might let you stay—mindin' you don't scare off my game."

We bandied back and forth, and he calmed down a mite. Again, I offered, "Mister Luster, let me fix you somethin' nice an' warm to drink."

"Granny, I ain't gonna stand here palaverin' no longer. I'm warnin' you one last time—keep this little section o'

the mountain quiet, or else." He lifted the shotgun he was carryin' and waved the barrel in my face, threatenin'–like.

Then that giant of a man turned 'round and spit—yessir, he spit right at my feet.

"Why, Mister Luster, that 'tain't very friendly," I said, complainin'. He laughed—hard and hateful—so much it set my teeth to chattering. Then he started walkin' away.

His puppy dog just sat there, cowerin'. Luster turned back, saw the dog still sittin', and snarled, "Come on, Shep, git over here—right now!"

That little hound jumped up and follered ol' Luster into the the woods.

I watched the back of that ornery giant as he disappeared, and somethin' my grandpappy told me came to mind. "Little girl," he used to say, "you can catch more flies with honey than you ever can with vinegar." I remember thinkin' that was pretty silly, but suddenly, it seemed right smart. I knew then what he meant. I'm gonna tame me a fly—no sir, not a fly—with the Lord's help, I'm gonna tame me a giant, ol' cockroach.

So, I moseyed back into my little cabin and took down a jar of plum-blossom jelly.

Come next mornin', I rose just as the sun pushed its face over the hills, and songbirds greeted the dawn. I headed up the mountain to where I saw smoke curlin' from a stovepipe. Sure enough, I came to this lean-to that'd once belonged to an old man who'd died many years back. That shack was more layin' down than it was standin' up—mighty tired it was.

Steppin' near the door, I called out, "Howdy, Luster—howdy, Mr. Luster." I heard a-rattlin' and a-stompin'. That board actin' like a door opened suddenly and banged the side of the shack.

"What you think you're doin' up here? I told you I don't like nobody gettin' in my way. Git out afore I fill you with buckshot."

"Now, Mr. Luster, that's no way to talk," I said. "I just intended to be kinda neighborly. I brought you some real sweet plum-blossom jelly."

"Don't want no jelly, don't want no neighbors. Jist leave me be, ya hear?"

I set that jar of jelly down on the dirt and stepped back.

"Yes, sir, I'll go if that's how you feel. Lord loves you anyway, Mr. Luster."

"Git outta here!" bellowed the giant.

Granny picked up the Mason jar and poured more chicory into Pete's cup. "You still wantin' to hear this?" she asked.

The boy nodded.

"Well, Pete, I tell you, things went on like that most o' the summer."

The old woman stopped talking, brushed a strand of gray hair back from her forehead, and tilted her head, listening. From somewhere high in the trees, an owl hooted, soft and low.

"Thank ya," she whispered, nodding toward the sound. Then, with a faint sigh, she continued.

Sometimes I'd see Luster and his dog, but when I tried to say "Howdy," he'd jist spit 'n' turn the other way. Little ol' Shep kept trailin' right there at the big man's heels. They looked like two of the loneliest souls the good Lord ever created.

People in the village talked about Luster, but I didn't pay 'em no mind. Some said he's a criminal, others that he's violent—some even said he's as loco as a jay eatin' fo-mented berries. I even heard tell that maybe he killed a

man. But Luster and I kept out of each other's way. I just prayed a little harder:

"Lord, I know you been watchin' out for me—and you made that Luster. Somethin' musta hurt that man real bad for him to be so hateful. You're just gonna have to help him—'cause I'm sure stayin' far away and mindin' my own business."

Well, the days and weeks and months, they sailed on. One afternoon on Christmas Eve day, storm clouds came rollin' in, and snow fell in big, lacy flakes. Then, sudden–like, the temperature dropped, and icicles formed from my roof.

In my little cabin, the pot–belly stove was burnin' warm and steady. I snuggled down as puffs of snow drifted through the chinks in the walls and settled in sugary mounds around the room, restin' on the table and floor afore meltin' into tiny puddles.

Feelin' mighty grateful, I rocked in my chair, thinkin' about my blessin's. I had my health, and I had my little house—and that was more than enough.

Hours passed, and I began ponderin' on those who didn't have the blessin's I had. Then a thought started tappin' on my mind, remindin' me of Luster, sittin' up there in his fallin'–down shack, all alone except for his dawg.

There was a sorta nudge on my heart, and I argued right out loud. "Oh, no, Lord, there's nothin' I can do. Why, that man's so mean, and his heart's so small, that you gotta take one o' those magnifyin' glasses and hold it up real high to see if he even has a heart. Not sure you'd see it then."

Still, those thoughts didn't stop. They kept badgerin' me.

"Okay," says I, right out loud, "if you insist. I reckon you're tellin' me it's not right for someone to be alone and forgotten on your special night."

So I took a clean towel and wrapped a loaf o' warm bread just out o' the cast-iron spider. Then I hauled down a poke o' walnuts I'd been savin' and set everything in a basket. Liftin' my ol' wool coat from the nail, I put it on and tossed a worn blanket over my head to keep off the bitin' chill.

It took a while to trudge through the snowdrifts and up the high ridge to where Luster lived. I was tremblin' as I stood outside his door and called, "Oh, Luster! Howdy, Mr. Luster—I got a Christmas present for you."

Granny paused, eyes widened, as if seeing it all over again.

"Pete," she whispered, "this is where things got downright frightenin'. I never in my whole life heard such an explosion. Why, it was near as loud as when them highway fellers were blastin' through the pass with dynamite."

That Luster came barrelin' out with the worst rage I've ever seen on a human face.

"I won't stand for no talk about Christmas," he bellowed. "Don't you ever come here again, Granny! You're lucky I'm cleanin' my shotgun, an' it ain't loaded. You mark my words—next time, I'll shoot!"

For a moment, I couldn't move. My voice squeaked, and I don't rightly know where it came from, but I heard myself say, "The Lord loves ya just the same, Mr. Luster."

The giant slammed the shack door so hard I was surprised the place didn't fall. I set the basket on a snowbank and scuttled back down the mountain to my holler as fast as I could go. On the way, I was prayin', "You gotta touch that ol' Luster's heart, 'cause I've got no way o' talkin' to him."

Soon after I reached my little place, it got dark. I put more wood in the stove and busied myself stirrin' oatmeal for supper. The wind picked up and started creepin' through the cracks and callin' at my window. It howled and howled.

"Pete, you can't imagine what happened next!" Granny's voice faded into the hush of the snowy night. She turned to see if the boy was still listening.

Pete sat motionless, his eyes wide, catching the glint of starlight reflected on the snow.

"Don't stop, Granny," he whispered. "Please—what happened then?"

I heard voices—they was yellin' an' callin'. I thought I must be dreamin'. Soon, there was poundin' on my door.

"Granny, Granny—open up!"

I opened the door, and the sheriff and some fellers from the village stood shiverin' on my sittin' porch, snow dustin' their hats and coats.

"Granny, we need your help," said the sheriff. "Could you fix a pot o' chicory and let these boys come in to warm up a spell. Down the mountain a piece, where the old blacktop hits the pass, there's been a terrible accident. Rockslides've blocked the road."

"Oh no," I said, my heart racin'. "What happened? Course I'll help. Come on in! Come on in!"

"A young couple, likely blinded by the snow and all, crashed their car right into those boulders," the sheriff explained. "The man's unconscious, and the woman's out of her mind. She keeps screamin' and cryin' out, 'Sandy, Sandy.' No way could anyone give that girl peace. The ambulance got 'em out and headed toward Gatlinburg just afore that road was blocked."

The old woman paused, rubbing her eyes. The young woodcutter sat quiet, staring out into the snow. After a long moment, Granny drew a deep breath and went on.

Then the sheriff said somethin' that plumb tore my heart right out.

"Granny, the real sad part is—in the back seat of what's left of their car, we found a baby doll, a raggedy old teddy bear—even some broken-up cookies. Little bitty tracks headed up the mountain, lookin' like they was comin' this way. We tried to follow, but the snow's covered 'em up."

The woman's voice caught, and she paused again.

"There's a young'un lost on the mountain," the sheriff went on. "The boys an' me've been out lookin'. It's gettin' mighty cold now, and truth be, there ain't much hope o' findin' a child alive. Most likely froze by now—or taken by coyotes or the like. But we gotta keep tryin'. So, if you don't mind, we need you to keep a pot o' chicory hot, so my men can thaw out once an' again."

Fightin' tears, I said, "Why, sure, I'll keep the pot a-boilin'. Poor little mite. It's terrible any time—but Christmas? It's just not right."

After the men drank a couple cups apiece and trudged back out into the cuttin' cold, I started thinkin' and prayin'.

"Lord, you know all about that young couple and their poor little one."

Then, clear as sunrise, a notion settled hard on my heart.

"Why yes… there's one ol' man who's strong enough. Why yes… there's one ol' man who's tough enough. And yes, there's one ol' man who knows this mountain—and he's got hisself a huntin' dog. If anyone can find that child, that Luster can."

Then I remembered.

"Well, Lord, you're gonna have ta help me. Luster told me he'd blast my head off if'n I came 'round his shack again. So if you're wantin' me to go there, I reckon you'll have ta put a cork in his gun. But I'll do what ya say."

Pete sat there, eyes wide.

"But Granny," said the boy, "weren't ya scared?"

"'Course I was," said the old woman, "but what else could I do?"

I tugged on my old boots, slid into my sweater and coat, then grabbed my blanket wrap and walkin' stick. The snow was fallin' so heavy it was hard to see. Winds blew and tore, almost knockin' me off my feet, but I finally got to Luster's shack.

"Yes sirree, Pete—I was shakin'," she said with a soft chuckle. "I reckon I was nervous as a cat in a room full o' rockers."

"Howdy, Luster! Mr. Luster!" I hollered.

I waited, expectin' him to come out blastin'—but didn't hear a thing. I called again.

"Please don't shoot, Mr. Luster—I gotta talk to you. Someone needs your help."

Still no answer.

I cautiously pushed the door open and jumped back. "Lord, you go first," I said. "I don't mean ta be rude."

Finally, I stepped inside—weren't nobody there.

I looked around. "Whoo–ee," I muttered, "sure is a mess. Don't reckon that man knows how to pick up anythin'."

I wandered over to a broken-down shelf, where an old yellowed photograph sat of a pretty young woman holdin' a blonde, curly-headed little boy. Beside it lay a pair of moth–eaten silk gloves and a raggedy toy dog.

"Lord," I whispered, "looks like you're showin' me that ol' Luster's been hurtin' a long time. But we'll be hurtin', too, if we don't get outta here afore he gets back."

Pullin' the door shut behind me, I stepped out into the deep snow, carryin' more questions than I got answers.

Just as I started down the trail, I saw Shep—Luster's little dog—strugglin' through the drifts. I looked and looked, 'spectin' to see Luster. For a moment, I wondered if this Christmas Eve was gonna be my night to fly to heaven.

I patted Shep's head. He took hold of my sleeve and tugged.

"What you doin'?" I scolded. "I got no time to play. I gotta go home, stoke the fire, and keep the pot a-boilin' in case those men come back. Shoo now, Shep! Let loose!"

But that dog—he held on.

Finally, I realized he was coaxin' me to go with him, so I went along.

I slipped on rocks hidin' under the snow. Slush and ice seeped down into my boots, and freezin' wind blasted beneath my coat and blanket.

Once, I fell flat on my backside, spun, then slid a few feet like a june bug in a windstorm.

I follered that little dog down the mountainside, where the rocks were so steep I had trouble stayin' on my feet.

Suddenly, the storm quieted. The snow stopped fallin'. The wind hushed. And the sky opened clear, filled with a million stars.

The Christmas star shone so bright, it near took my breath. There, in its vast glory, was a Bethlehem sky.

Shep raced on ahead and started diggin' at a mound of snow drifted against a huge rock. He poked his nose in, snorted, then put both paws on somethin' and commenced to cryin' and whinin' like a baby.

"Shep, no time for huntin'," I scolded.

Then I saw what that pup was doin'. He was lyin' on the chest of a man—a great big man.

"Luster! Luster!" I screamed, but Luster didn't answer— Luster didn't move—Luster didn't breathe.

With tremblin' hands, I gently wiped the snow from his forehead, cheeks, and mouth. Two icy rivers, frozen solid, ran from his eyes, leavin' shiny trails down to his beard.

There, in the light of the Christmas star, with those tears frozen on his face, Luster looked different. He didn't look mean. He didn't look hateful. He didn't even look dirty.

Then I noticed Luster wasn't wearin' a coat. His heavy ol' sheepskin was drawn up tight against his massive chest. His arms were folded over it, kinda protective–like, holdin' it close to his heart.

I sat there starin', and then that coat stirred just a mite.

Pushin' Shep aside, I unfolded Luster's arms and opened the sheepskin. There inside, warm as a kitten in a haystack, was a little curly–headed girl.

So I wrapped the young'un tight in Luster's coat, and that little dog and I took her down the mountain.

Come next mornin', Christmas Day and all, the men from the village fetched the body of the big man and carried him back up to the holler near his shack, where they reverently laid him to rest.

"After that, Pete, Shep came to live with me. And every year, come Christmas Eve, while I'm down at the Nativity service in the little church in the village, that ol' dog finds his way back up yonder to Luster's shack."

The old woman's voice softened as she lifted her gaze to the bright star overhead.

"I reckon now you understand why I believe in miracles. It's not anythin' near the same as the miracle of Jesus' birth, but it sure feels like a miracle to me."

She tipped her head, listening. "Hear that? The bells are ringin' for service. We've been sittin' far too long."

Rising to her feet, Granny looked into the young woodcutter's face. Reaching out, she gently wiped the tears from his eyes.

"Now, Pete, don't you be givin' up. Sometimes we don't even see 'em while they're happenin', but Christmastime truly is a season of miracles."

Lucille MacDermaid
1921 – 2022

Dorothy Haley
1922 – 2003

Author's Note

Miracle on the Mountain: An Appalachian Christmas began as a Christmas monologue for a church and community gathering organized by my mother, Lucille MacDermaid. At first, I said no when she asked me to give the program—but, as always, she knew I'd come around.

I wrote the piece on a long drive to visit our daughter at college, speaking into a mini tape recorder with only a flicker of an idea. That's when Granny's voice came to me— inspired by Dorothy Haley, my mother's cousin and lifelong friend. Her gentle Kentucky accent and quiet strength became the heart of this story.

On the night of the performance, I walked into the church in an old flannel coat, powdered white hair, calling for Shep. The story unfolded with memory, music, and laughter. When it ended, the audience softly sang "Silent Night." My mother beamed. Dorothy, with tears in her eyes, hugged me and whispered,

"Oh, Gaily, you took me right back home."

That's when I knew this story was meant to be shared.

I dedicate this book to both of them—with love.

About the
Author

Gail Heath is the author and illustrator of several children's books, including the Accelerated Reader title *Inside Me, Sometimes*. Growing up as the daughter of a U.S. Air Force officer, she lived all over the world—from Japan, Germany, and France to many U.S. cities—always with a story in her heart and a book in her hands.

A lifelong educator with degrees from Michigan State University and Central Michigan University, Gail's work has appeared in magazines, anthologies, and newspapers. She has received the Will Rogers Silver Medallion Award and a Santa Barbara Writers Conference Award.

Through her stories, Gail hopes to inspire young readers to be curious, kind, and confident while celebrating the beauty of diversity.

About the
Illustrator

Barabash Sviatoslav was born in Kovel, Ukraine, and discovered his passion for drawing at sixteen. He trained at Odessa Art College and the National Academy of Painting in Kyiv, completing fourteen years of study. A member of the Union of Artists of Ukraine, he has exhibited widely.

Inspired by his grandfather, Alexander Manelyuk, a graphic designer, Sviatoslav's work combines traditional painting with digital art to create vibrant, textured illustrations. For *Miracle on the Mountain: An Appalachian Christmas,* he captured the story's warmth and timeless mountain spirit.